ANTHONY'S ADVENTURES

Already a Winner!

Dr. Brenda Everett Mitchell

ANTHONY'S ADVENTURES

Already a Winner!

ISBN: 978-0-578-73531-3

Printed in the United States of America.

Executive Book Coach - Dr. Gail Hayes, Handle Your Business Girl Publishing

DEDICATION

I dedicate this book to the men in my life, my sons Wayne Anthony and William and to my husband Glenn. Thank you for your loving support. Special thanks also to my encouraging family and friends who have, over the years, watched me journal about events in Wayne Anthony's life. Thank you to my sisters Gwendolyn and Tekeisha for giving me wonderful feedback to make this book the best ever. A special thanks to my grandson, Jayden, nephews Alan and Ian, and to my nieces Corrine and Makayla, who read the book and loved it!

This book is also dedicated to Precious, a 1-year-old boy who I met in Malawi. His mother, Triza's bravery astounded me and prompted me to write this book. Precious is in therapy with Titi Titus and is making progress with his sensory deficits.

I also extend my heartfelt thanks to the Women of the Word (WOW) Sunday School class of Union Baptist Church of Durham. Your loving spiritual and financial support is a blessing for Precious and other children with albinism in Malawi.

This book also honors the bravery and persistence of individuals with albinism all over the world and especially Malawi as they have traditionally been misunderstood resulting in mistreatment by others. As we view current world events of protests by individuals advocating for racial justice and equality, we must stand and raise our collective voices to end discrimination of all kinds. I'm especially grateful for the outstanding work that my friend, Titi Titus Mwanjabe (OT), is doing to bridge two countries as he and his team provide rehabilitation therapy. Although his days are full, he and Maynard Zacharia invest their personal time to assist other individuals with albinism.

I DON'T WANT TO GO!

"*Okay, here comes the sun,*" Anthony thought as he slowly turned over in his bed. The sunshine peeked through the window shades and his room felt warm. It was as if the sun had fingers and they were trying to open the shades and the window. The sunlight, although it was beautiful, was not his friend. He was a boy with albinism - albinism and sunshine don't mix.

He and the sun were not good friends. He knew that sunlight made the flowers and trees to grow, but if he went outside without his sunscreen, the sun would burn his skin and hurt his eyes. He looked at the bottle of sunscreen on his dresser and remembered his sunglasses on the table by the front door. He knew he had to use both before he went outside.

"I am not going today. I don't feel like fighting Brandon for a seat on the bus or dealing with other school mates who ask me a million questions like - why do you look that way? Why do you wear sunglasses outside? Are you Black or White? Why are you putting on sunscreen?"

 "There is always drama and I don't want any part of it! That stuff makes me sad because I really like going to school and making good grades."

"Come on Anthony! We have to eat and catch the bus," said his brother Evan while throwing a pillow at him playfully. He was already dressed and ready to go.

Anthony got up and put on his school uniform, combed his hair, and rubbed on his sunscreen. He looked in the mirror and shrugged his shoulders because he didn't want to go!

The smell of breakfast floated in the air and his growling stomach told him that it was time to face the world. When he came downstairs, he could feel his mother's smile.

"If only I had super powers! That way, I could make everybody leave me alone!" Anthony thought as he prepared to go downstairs. He wondered if there was something to protect him from bullies like Brandon. Just the thought of him irritated Anthony.

"Good morning sleepy head. I made your favorite," she said as she hugged and kissed him on the forehead. Anthony playfully tried to pull away but she never let him escape. He acted irritated but he secretly loved her hugs and kisses - they got him through his day.

"The last one to the bus is a rotten egg!" Evan shouted as he ran to the bus. But this morning, Anthony didn't care about racing because he knew the battle was about to begin. Anthony quickly ate his breakfast and walked towards the front door checking to be sure that he had all of his homework and school supplies. As he nervously smiled at his mother, she gave him one last hug and his lunch bag. He put on his sunglasses, cap and picked up his book bag while Evan raced out the door ahead of him.

Anthony crossed the street to get on the bus dreading the 5 mile ride to school. He wanted to be happy to go to school but it was so hard. He even thought about asking his mother to take him to school so he wouldn't have to deal with the bad kids on the bus.

YOU CAN'T SIT HERE!

As Anthony came to the bus, he took a deep breath before he climbed the steps. He held his shoulders back and his head up. But as he got on the bus, he realized that his bravery act did not work because there was no place for him to sit. Evan had already found a seat and was busy talking to his friend Aiden.

"Find a seat Anthony," the bus driver said as he closed the door. But Anthony felt like a giant icicle frozen to the bus floor. He could see Brandon was alone in a seat and had his book bag beside him near the window. Anthony slowly moved down the aisle and stood beside the seat, waiting for Brandon to move over.

"I know you're not waiting to sit in my seat. Go, somewhere else and sit," Brandon said as he turned and glared at Anthony. Anthony could hear some of the other children laugh as he stood there trembling. It was as if he could feel fear and anger tapping him on the shoulder. All he wanted to do was move Brandon and his bag and sit down. He didn't have a name for what he felt but as he stood there, something was holding him back from doing it. So, all he did was stand there waiting and afraid to even see if there really was another seat for him to sit down.

"But there's no other seat," Anthony said as his words almost got caught in his throat. He stood there hoping that Brandon would move, but inside, he knew better. He looked around for help and realized that the bus driver was talking to some other people at the front of bus.

"Brandon, move over or sit with Franklin!" Anthony heard Evan's voice. He was so focused on what was happening that he didn't realize that Evan was standing beside him.

"Give up the seat so us brothers can sit together," Evan said. Brandon looked at Evan's face and he could tell from the tone of his voice that he was serious. No one wanted to tangle with Evan. Although he was little, he was fierce.

"I had this seat first and if you don't like it, you can…" Brandon said.

"Move over Brandon or get another seat so we can get to school," the bus driver's voice cut through the air like a sword. Evan stood beside the seat and his frown turned into a grin. Brandon grabbed his bag and quickly moved to another seat. By this time, Anthony was deep in his own world. All he could think about was escaping and building a wall around himself with his Legos.

"Don't worry brother. I got you!" Evan said as he slid onto the seat next to him. Evan continued talking as if nothing happened, but Anthony couldn't hear a word he said. His mind was in another place. Although it was nice to have his brother stand up for him, Anthony was not happy. He was the older brother. He should have been the one standing up to Brandon. He tried to ignore how he was feeling but Anthony knew that on most mornings, Brandon and his friends, Collin and Ian, would block seats and not let others sit with them.

They would pick and choose who sat where on the bus. Every morning, one of them would block him from sitting down. There was always the bus seat battle. One morning, things got rough because Brandon and another boy named Eddie almost got into a fight.

I JUST CAN'T THINK STRAIGHT!

That day, school was a blur. People whispering and asking questions didn't bother him. He could barely focus on his work because he was thinking about getting on the bus going home. Even though his mother made his favorite lunch, Anthony couldn't eat it all. He just took a few bites and threw the rest away. He didn't notice any of those things that usually bothered him because his mind was still focused on how he could stand up to Brandon. All he could think about was how he no longer wanted Evan to be his protector. He wanted to become the older brother who didn't need protection.

He usually loved being at school and was a good student. But even going to his favorite classes didn't help him forget what he knew he had to face, He wasn't sure why Brandon always picked on him but he had to find a way to make it stop. It seemed like the more he thought about making it stop, the more angry and afraid he became.

That afternoon, Anthony was already on the bus when Brandon and his gang arrived. They were busy talking about things that happened at school and tried to talk to him, but he didn't hear their words. They even tried to get him to move from his seat, but that didn't work either. All the way home, he ignored everyone because he was still embarrassed and angry. He didn't even talk to Evan.

He could hear everyone around him talking and laughing but he did not join in. All he could think about was going to his room and being alone so he could read one of his books or build a wall with his Legos.

WHY CAN'T I STAND UP TO HIM?

"Hey, are you alright?" Evan asked, as they were getting off the bus. Instead of answering, Anthony literally ran to the front door. When they got inside, he looked past Evan to see if the way was clear for him to just run up the stairs to their bedroom. He didn't answer his brother because he was too angry. As Evan turned away and walked towards the kitchen, he heard his mother's voice.

"Anthony, we've got snacks in the kitchen. Are you coming?"

"No, Mom. I don't want a snack," he said as he headed up the stairs. He could hear his mother's footsteps as she walked towards the stairs so he hurried to his room because he just didn't want her to ask about his day. He just couldn't talk to her or anyone. He had been holding back his tears all day and he didn't want her to see him cry. He knew that would be the start of another conversation.

He knew that once he got to his room and closed the door, he could let them come. He dropped his book bag on the floor and threw himself on the bed, buried his face in his pillow and cried. After he cried for a few minutes, he got up and walked towards his mirror. He wiped away his tears, and just stared at himself in the mirror. He was still so angry that he couldn't talk..

"*Why can't I stand up to Brandon? Why does he always bother me? Why can't he find someone else to pick on? If Evan can stand up to him, then I should be able to do it too*," he thought. He wiped his eyes and just stared in the mirror for a minute. As he turned to walk away, he thought he saw a glimmer of light in the mirror but he thought he was just seeing things. He hesitated for a minute and convinced himself that there was nothing there.

WHAT IN THE WORLD?

"So, you tired of cryin' yet?" A strange voice interrupted his thoughts and surprised Anthony. He knew what he heard because he had great hearing but he didn't see anyone. He took a long look around just to make sure he was still alone.

"I'm in the mirror right in front of you," said the voice. "So, I'm gonna ask you again, are you tired of cryin' yet?" As he stared at the mirror, it seemed like his eyesight was very clear but he kept blinking his eyes to make sure he was seeing what he was seeing.

"Yeah, you're seeing right. It's me in the mirror," the voice said. Anthony slowly moved closer to the mirror to take a closer look. He was secretly hoping that Evan didn't come into the room. He didn't want his brother to think that he was losing it. As Anthony stared in the mirror, he saw bright flashes of color. He squinted his eyes to focus just to make sure he wasn't just seeing things.

"Look, I know you can see me so you can stop the squinting 'cause you don't need to do that. Now that I finally got your attention. Everything with me should be very clear, even your vision. I'm here in living color and I got lots to say to you! So, stop staring and just listen!"

Anthony could barely believe what he was seeing but what he was seeing was real. As he looked in the mirror, he realized that he didn't need to squint. He could see this figure in bright, clear, living color! He was just as surprised by his clear eyesight as he was about this strange person talking to him in his mirror.

"Listen man, you can't go on like this, so I thought I'd step in 'cause you need some help. You need help, don't you?" he asked. Anthony was stunned but he still nodded his head in agreement.

"I know everything about you. I know every thought and every feeling. You know why? Because, I am you! Take a look at us. We have the same hair. We have the same arms and hands. We have the same ears and we have the same voice. Can't you see? Can't you hear it? We are the same. Only thing different is that I KNOW I'm super. You still got work to do!" Super Antney laughed.

"There's something I need you to do. Come closer and take a good, long look at me," Super Antney said. As Anthony gazed into the mirror, all he could see was this person wearing a bright T-shirt with a bottle of sunscreen on his chest. He was wearing a cap like the ones that he liked to wear. And the strangest thing he noticed was that this "Super Antney" was wearing a cape!

"But who are you? How do you know me? How do you know what I need? Are you real? How did you get inside my mirror?" Anthony asked nervously. He had so many questions and it seemed that they all came out all at once.

"Stop asking so many questions. I'm gonna answer all of them but first things first. Let me introduce myself. My name is, now don't forget this, Super Antney! Man, I am really super! And do you know why? Cause I got the answers to your problems!"

"I…don't understand. Why are you…" Anthony said as he continued blinking. He was still in a state of shock because he could actually see and hear this person clearly.

"Just look, listen and don't talk. I know this may be a little hard for you, but we don't have much time before Evan comes up here," interrupted Super Antney. Anthony stood frozen for a moment.

"What's up with this guy? He's more lame than I am. He's wearing a cape!" Anthony thought. He realized that what he was seeing was real and this person in the mirror looked familiar and he even knew Evan!

"So you think I'm lame, huh? Well, take a look. Who's wearing the cape, me or you? Besides, who's scared of Brandon, me or you?"

Whaaat? How do you know about Brandon? How do you know what I'm thinking?" asked Anthony. Anthony wasn't sure if he liked this cape wearing smart guy, but he did have a point. As he stared in the mirror at Super Antney, he could see that they did look a lot alike. They were the same height. They had the same face and even the same hair. They did talk alike, except this Super Antney guy talked more than he did. He did not like that Super Antney was laughing at him.

"Are you ready to talk now and see how we can work together to help you with this Brandon situation? Hey, if you don't like me laughing at you, then you need to listen up! We don't have all day,"   Super Antney said.

DON'T LET FEAR RULE YOU!

"Yep, that's right! It's time you stood up to this guy. I can tell you that once you stand up to him, no one else on the bus will bother you. But that is all up to you. I can help you, if you will listen."

"Okay, so what do I do? When I see him, how do I stop my knees from shaking?" asked Anthony.

"So, before I answer that, let me ask you a couple of questions. When you put together your math, how do you finish it? Who helps you? When you get dressed every day, who dresses you? When you eat your breakfast, who picks up your spoon to feed you? I know you use a spoon 'cause I know you like cereal. When you come home, who carries you up the stairs?"

"I could ask you a million questions and the answer would still be the same. It's you! If you can do all those things on your own, then you can stand up to this Brandon and his gang, on your own. You are more powerful than you believe my Man! They only do what they do because you let them do what they do. Have you noticed how easy it was for Evan and Eddie to stand up to these guys?"

"Believe it or not, there is just one thing you need to remember when it comes to dealing with these guys. Man, you can't let fear rule you! Remember, you can't lose because you are a winner! You win every day when you get up in the morning. Tomorrow is going to be different because we're gonna make sure it is! Repeat after me, I can't lose because I am already a winner! Your turn! Come on! Once you say the words, fear's gotta run! Fear can't stay in a place where courage is in charge!" Super Antney said as he stared at Anthony.

I CAN'T LOSE!

"I CAN'T LOSE BECAUSE I'M ALREADY A WINNER! I CAN'T LOSE BECAUSE I'M ALREADY A WINNER!" Anthony said with a voice louder than even he had ever heard. The more he said it, the more powerful he felt.

"Why are you yelling?" Evan said, as he burst into the room. "I could hear you all the way down the hall. It's time to eat. Are you okay brother?" Anthony smiled when he saw his little brother's face. He admired Evan more than he knew and he always felt better when they were together. He wanted to be the big brother he believed Evan deserved and he was ready do something to make that happen.

"I'm fine Evan. I just felt like yelling," Anthony said as he sat on the bed and took off his shoes.

"I'm sorry about what happened with Brandon. He's a mean guy. One day, I believe you will stand up to him and when you do, he will leave you alone." Evan said as he turned to leave the room.

"Hey Anthony! Look at me and listen," said Super Antney. "People like Brandon are more scared than you are. If you ever decide to stand up to him, you will find out just how scared he really is."

All he could do was to think about how in one day his life had changed. He felt like he finally met someone who knew how he felt. It was funny but he believed that he made a new and different kind of friend, and he didn't even have to leave his room to talk to his new friend!

"Hey, it looks like you're feeling better," his mother said as she said goodnight to them. Before she could say another word, Anthony rushed towards her and gave her a big hug. She did not need words to let her know how he felt. His hug was enough.

As they brushed their teeth, he looked in the bathroom mirror at his little brother and was so happy to have him in his life. He could see their differences but they were brothers and nothing could change that.

I LIKE WHO I AM

When he compared Evan's dark brown skin and his light skin, he wondered how they could look so different but be so alike. He knew that Albinism caused them to look different, but they were still brothers. So if Evan could be brave, he could too. Evan was his best friend. They liked so many of the same things. They shared the same room and they could tell what the other was thinking and they laughed at the same things.

He went to bed believing that the next day was going to be different. It had to be different because he was different. It was going to be a day that he could prove that he was now brave. At least that's what he hoped would happen. That night, Anthony slept better than he had in many days.

"Hey boy, it's time to get up! You can't sleep all day," Anthony yelled while waking up Evan. Evan sat up in his bed and just stared. This was the first time that he could remember that Anthony woke him up for school and it startled him.

"Hey Brother, are you okay? I'm the one who wakes you up. What's goin' on?" asked Evan with a shocked look on his face. He also had a slight smile on his face because he could see that his big brother was in a good mood.

"I just feel good today. Anyway, I need to wake up my little brother sometime, don't I?" Anthony said with a big smile that Evan had not seen in a long time. This good mood made Evan happy too and he jumped up and quickly got dressed. He was both surprised and hungry.

"I'll see you downstairs," Evan said as he left the room. Anthony was in no hurry to follow him. He needed one more thing before he went downstairs.

"Hey, Super Antney! You there?" Anthony said as he stared at his mirror.

"You know I am. So, what do you want? I already told you what you need to do, so go do it! I don't need to tell you again!" Super Antney said as he disappeared from the mirror. Anthony knew that everything was up to him. He was already a winner so he believed that he couldn't lose.

When he got on the bus, Anthony was nervous, but he knew that once he confronted Brandon, everything would be different.

Have you ever been afraid of someone? Think about it for a minute. If you have, then you have 2 choices. Can you name them? Let's see if Anthony makes the right choice and listens to me and stands up to Brandon!

LOOK OUT BRANDON! HERE I COME!

"What if Brandon bothers me? What am I going to say? What am I going to do? Maybe he won't pay attention to me because he will be sitting in the back with his friends again. Maybe that's where he'll stay from now on," thought Anthony. He could feel fear tapping him on the shoulder and he tried not to pay attention. As he got on the bus, he saw Evan already in a seat talking. The only open seat was with, you guessed it, Brandon!

"You know you can't sit here, right?" Brandon said as he stared at Anthony and then turned towards the window. Anthony took a deep breath and could see Evan getting up from his seat.

"I can't lose because I'm already a winner. I can't lose because I'm already a winner!" Anthony's inner voice reminded him of his conversation with Super Antney.

"Brandon, move over and move your book bag! I need to sit down!" Anthony's loud voice caught everyone off guard! He could feel everyone watching and everything on the bus stopped.

"I got this brother," Anthony said as he looked at Evan and motioned for him to sit down. Evan's facial expression was priceless and Anthony's knees were knocking so hard that he thought everyone could hear them. But he knew this was his moment of bravery and nothing was going to stop it.

"Well, what you gonna do? **I NEED TO SIT DOWN SO WE CAN GET TO SCHOOL!**" Anyone could tell that Brandon was shocked. No one, including Evan had ever heard Anthony shout this loudly before.

Even the bus driver, who was about to step in, just watched and smiled. Then something miraculous happened. Brandon moved over without saying a word! He put his book bag on his lap and moved over to the window seat. He didn't even look at Anthony but just stared out the window.

As Anthony slid into his seat, it felt like his heart was going to jump out of his chest. If this was how winning felt, he wanted to win a lot more. To him, what just happened was a miracle. He won a battle before it got started.

He got his seat on his own without Evan's help. This was a day he would long remember because he realized he could stand up for himself and be the big brother Evan deserved. The bus ride was quiet. Anthony had a hard time sitting still. As soon as the bus stopped, he jumped up and nearly ran to his classroom. That day, school was a breeze. He happily ate his lunch and even talked with his class-mates. Every time he thought about what happened on the bus, he smiled. The biggest surprise was that he didn't have trouble finding a seat on the bus!

"Anthony couldn't wait to end his school day to get back home and to his room. His mom greeted him by asking "How was your day?" He almost didn't hear her question when he came into his house be-cause he was so excited.

"It was good Mom," he said as he ran up the stairs. Evan came in the door behind him, but he did not follow Anthony upstairs. He was still stunned about what he had just seen and heard on the bus. Once Anthony got to his room, he threw his book bag on the bed and leaped in front of the mirror.

"Super Antney, you there? I got something to tell you. It's important," Anthony said, while trying to

catch his breath. He stood there for what seemed like forever and still did not see or hear Super Antney. "Super Antney, I need to talk to you. Where are you? I got to tell you what happened today. It's important!"

"I'm here. Whatcha want Man? I been waitin' all day and you finally showed up," Super Antney said as he interrupted Anthony. He had a big smile on his face. "What's so important that you can't breathe? Slow down Man. We got time!"

"Well, I did it! I stood up to Brandon. I told him to move and he gave me a seat on the bus."

"Man, you act like he did something special for you. Well, he didn't. He did what you told him to do and you got your seat. What's so special about that?"

"Why are you talking to me like that? You act like what happened to me…"

"Oh, I know what you did! What you did wasn't so special. It's the way you shoulda been actin' all along. You just needed somebody to help you find the courage to do it. This thing has been inside of you the whole time Man, and I just did my job and helped you to see it!" Super Antney replied.

"Do you mean to tell me that I could have done this without you?"

Now, I didn't say that. Right now, we got to work together until you can do things on your own. Now, you got a good start. This is a piece of cake. But know this, I will be here if you need me and as long as you listen. Together, we can do some great things."

I GOT THE POWER!

Anthony stared at Super Antney and he saw something he hadn't noticed before. Super Antney had a familiar smile and even his hair was like his hair. They could almost be twins. It was as if he was looking at himself in the mirror. He finally realized what was going on with him and Super Antney!

"Do you have it yet? Yes, we look alike and we even think alike. I'm just not scared. You gotta work on that one 'cause it's bad for both of us! Today, you did good. We gonna get along fine if you listen and remember that your words have power. You form your thoughts with your words. If you say somethin', you gotta believe it! You used your power words today. That's how you won!"

"Power words?" Anthony asked. He had no idea what Super Antney was talking about. After the bus event, he was just happy to see his friend.

"Come on Man, you know your power words. You been thinkin' them all day. You been sayin' them all day long too! How many times do I have to tell you? So, let's say the words together so we both remember why we're here," Super Antney said. 'I got a job to do and my job is to help you, but you got a big part in this thing! Ready?"

Anthony stood there looking into Super Antney eyes and thought back on everything that happened that day. He remembered the words. He held his shoulders back, looked in the mirror and spoke. As he heard his own voice, he also heard Super Antney saying the words with him.

That day, Anthony realized that his battle that day had not been with just Brandon. His battle was with someone closer to him. It was with someone he talked to and saw every day. His battle was with himself and that day he won!

WHAT IS ALBINISM?

Albinism is a hereditary condition that results in a lack of pigmentation in the skin, hair and eyes." This inherited condition is characterized by a lack of the pigment melanin, resulting in pale skin, light hair, pale eyes and impaired vision. Both parents must carry the gene in order to pass it on, but they may not have albinism themselves. Although in Europe and North America approximately 1 in 20,000 people has albinism, the rates are higher in Africa, with about 1 in 1,400 occurrences in Tanzania. The term "Person with albinism" is preferred over "albino" as it puts the person ahead of their condition. – www.underthesamesun.com

There are unique challenges that may adversely impact Black and African Americans with albinism more than other racial/ethnic groups. These factors are their fair skin, light hair, hazel or bluish gray eyes, vision problems and sensitivity to light in comparison to others in that group. Caucasians with albinism are frequently able to "pass," and are unable to fathom the issues of Black and African Americans. Rejection from the larger black community, intra-family conflict and stress as well as bullying all of which may lead to social isolation for those with the disorder, are among the factors that may adversely impact this group, according to the National Organization for Albinism and Hypopigmentation (NOAH). https://www.albinism.org/

Aside from scientific studies on the subject, there are very few books that engage the subject matter. Violent attacks against persons with albinism due to the belief in the magical power this group possesses in East Africa, have increased national and international attention by groups such as NOAH and Under the Same Sun (UTSS).

TEACHING THEMES

Self Esteem

Why was Anthony feeling down about riding the bus to school?

Why was Anthony not wanting to go to school?

Communication

Why didn't Anthony tell his mother how he felt?

Why are we sometimes afraid to tell others what we want or need?

Is it hard for you to express yourself?

Advocacy and Bullying

What does it mean to advocate for something or someone?

Anthony's brother Evan, spoke up for him on the bus. How would that make you feel to have someone speak up to help you?

Isolation

Do you ever feel like no one understands you?

What do you do?

What made Anthony feel isolated and alone?

Differences

How are you different?

What can you do to celebrate your differences and share with others?

ABOUT THE AUTHOR

Dr. Brenda Everett Mitchell is an Associate Professor at the University of North Carolina at Chapel Hill. She is a Speech Language Pathologist who is passionate about mentoring young adults. She is also a consultant in the School of Medicine for diversity, equity and inclusion. She is an international communicator who regularly consults on diversity, equity and inclusion and student mentoring.

This book is a work of love for Dr. Mitchell. Her son Wayne Anthony has Albinism. Her family and friends encouraged her for many years as she kept a journal about events in Wayne Anthony's life. When the ophthalmologist told her at 3 months old that he would never see more than the Big E on the eye chart, she was determined to do all she could to make his life as special as God intended for it to be. She advocated for him until he was able to advocate for himself.

For speaking engagements, contact her at Evermitch@iCloud.com.

Made in the USA
Middletown, DE
13 January 2021